Othello Bach's Whoever Heard of a Fird?

Illustrated by Shann Hurst

This was my favorite book. I hope you enjoy it as much as I did.

Love

Cousin

Chris

www.whoeverheardofafird.com

CHOICE
BOOKS

Bach, Othello, 1941 -
     Whoever heard of a Fird?

Summary: The adventures of Fird - a magical creature who is part fish and part bird - as he and his friend search for his lost
     species.

     I. Hurst, Shannon, ill   II Title

ISBN -13: 978-1479333189
ISBN - 10: 1479333182

Printed in the U.S.A.   First Edition
Published by Choice Books

To my mother

To take full advantage of the Fird experience which includes several original songs, we recommend that you purchase the companion audio CD or listen to streaming versions of the music on:

www.whoeverheardofafird.com/music.html

Chapter One

Once there was a little fird—just an ordinary fird, part fish, part bird—and he wanted to find a herd of fird. But nobody had ever heard of a fird.

Now, this little fird was raised by a nest of dickens— just ordinary dickens, part dog, part chickens—but they'd never heard of a fird. Fird was the only fird they knew, and they loved him very much.

When Fird was just a baby fird, the dickens gave him a pet—Snyder Spider. Now, Snyder Spider was a hairy little spider whose hair hung from his crown to the ground all around. He wore a little red baseball cap and eight tiny tennis shoes.

Snyder Spider and Fird were the best of friends.

Lucille Dicken—a very motherly dicken—awakened each morning, dressed quietly, then woke up everyone else in the dicken house. She had a particularly nice way of doing this.

"Wake Up!"

Wake up in the morning!
Get up, sleepyheads;
Get up to the dawning.
Now get up, get out of bed!

Wake up in the morning,
Wake up! In the morn,
Get up to the dawning.
There's a new day being born.

Wake up, little children!
Wake up, sleepy heads,
Get up, everybody!
Now get up, get out of bed!

Go out! See the sunshine,
Go out! Feel the dew;
It's a lovely, lovely morning,
It was made just for you!

Don't wait until tomorrow!
It can't be the same!
And this special morning
Won't come your way again!

Of course, everyone woke up in a terrific mood. However, on this particular day, Fird decided it was time he and Snyder should go find a herd of fird. Fird wanted to know his fird family, and to know if he was firding right.

"Oh, please don't go!" begged the dickens. "We love you very much."

"Thank you," said Fird, "but it's time for me to find a herd of fird."

Lucille Dicken cried. "But Firdie, haven't you ever wondered why no dicken has ever left Dicken Mountain?"

Fird had to admit he had not. The truth was, Fird didn't even know the dickens lived on a mountain. The only thing he'd ever wondered about were firds... and why no one had ever heard of a fird.

"Well," Lucille Dicken warned, "you just can't leave the mountain. There are big, bad boogie monsters at the bottom!"

Fird's little fird heart skipped a little fird beat. He took a deep breath. "I'm sorry," he said, "but still, I have to go—even if I have to face the boogie monsters! I must find out where I came from, where I'm going, and what I'm supposed to be!"

Snyder Spider trembled and shook. He wasn't nearly as brave as Fird, and he couldn't have cared less what a fird was, or what it was meant to be.

However, Snyder did love Fird a lot, and would go anywhere with him, even if he didn't want to go. But Snyder couldn't talk, so no one ever knew for sure what he was thinking.

They usually knew what he was feeling, though, because Snyder giggled and laughed and quivered and shook and danced and hummed like everyone else.

So with lots of hugs and kisses for everyone and from everyone, Fird and Snyder took off to search for a herd of fird.

Chapter Two

The farther down the mountain they went, the better they felt. They loved the freedom and excitement! And before they knew it, they were skipping and dancing, rolling and tumbling; and Fird was singing for all the world to hear.

"I'm So Glad"

I'm so glad to just be me,
To be the me I want to be,
I'm so glad to finally be just me!

To go wherever I want to go,
And find out what I want know;
I'm so glad to finally be just me!

I'm excited and delighted,
And so glad that I decided
To break loose and really set me free!

No one else could make me do it,
Bite it off and make me chew it!
Hey, world! Aren't you glad to meet me?
Aren't you glad to greet me?

WOW!

I'll be so glad to find me,
I'll even look behind me!
I can't be far away it's true.
Hey, I can even feel it,
No one will ever steal it!
I'll just be me and you be you!
I'll be me, and you just be you, too!

But soon they were at the bottom of the mountain and the forest became so thick, it grew very dark and shadowy around them. They moved slowly and quietly now, afraid they might alert the big, bad boogie monsters.

They crept from tree to bush... from bush to tree... from tree to tree... from bush to bush.

Then suddenly a huge limb cracked behind them! With lightning speed, Snyder jumped on Fird's head and pretended to be a hairy hat.

Fird whirled around and stopped. He gasped. A gigantic monster stood just a few feet away! It snarled and took a slow giant step toward him.

Fird whimpered and backed away. Snyder trembled and wailed in his tiny spider voice.

"Gotcha!" A loud voice growled behind them!

"No!" screamed Fird. "Please don't hurt us!"

'Shhh!" hissed Snyder. He didn't like Fird saying *us*; he wanted the monsters to think Fird was alone.

Then one of the monsters grabbed Snyder!

"No! Please!" cried Fird. "Please don't hurt Snyder!"

The monster dangled Snyder over his huge, hungry-looking mouth. Then he dropped him onto his big wet tongue!

Snyder threw a terrible fit inside the monster's mouth. He poked and kicked, bit and hit, jumped and fought, until the monster's eyes crossed. Then, moaning, the monster opened his great mouth and rolled Snyder out to the end of his tongue. He twirled him around, spun him in the air, flipped him over his head and batted him with his foot. Snyder sailed like a wet, hairy ball. The monsters played catch with him.

"Hey," cried Fird. "Please, don't hurt him! He's my best friend!"

The monsters stopped and gaped at him.

"Hurt him?" they all asked at once.

"Why would we hurt him?"

Fird sputtered,

"Be-because you're big, bad boogie monsters!"

Suddenly, all the monsters looked very sad. "Well, we're big," they admitted, "but we're not bad. In fact, we're just plain old boogie monsters. All we do is boogie!"

And with that, they all started to dance.

"Boogie Monster Boogie"

We live in your mind, right there in your head!
But you'll never ever find us under your bed.
Just hang around and see what we really do-de-doodle-de-do!
So don't hesitate; we hate to wait; we've gotta great boogie for
you!
Yeah!

Boogie! Monsters like to boogie!
Oh, Boogie! Do a spooky woogie!
Yeah, Woogie! Wiggle your butoogie!
Yeah, Boogie, Jiggle your pazoogie!
Boogie, boogie this way, woogie, woogie that way,
Boogie woogie any way, Boogie woogie all day!
Boogie!

It looked like such fun, Fird and Snyder joined them, and they all boogied and boogied and boogied until they were all boogied out. Then they fell into a great hairy heap, laughing and trying to catch their breath.

"So what brings you into the woods today?" asked one of the monsters.

"I'm looking for a herd of fird," said Fird. "Have you seen any?"

Puzzled, the monsters all shook their huge heads. "What's a fird?"

"I'm a fird," said Fird, "Part fish, part bird, and I'm looking for a herd of fird."

"Hmmm," said one of the monsters. "Nope. We've never even heard of a fird. But if we do, we'll tell it you're looking for it."

"Thanks," said Fird. He and Snyder left, waving goodbye. The monsters all wiggled their big behinds, and said, "Come back and boogie sometime!"

Snyder wiggled his tiny behind and waved his cap.

"Wow," Fird said, as they continued through the forest, "it's too bad the dickens never left the mountain to meet the monsters, isn't it?

Snyder nodded.

"They have spent their whole life being afraid of something they've never met!" Fird added.

Chapter Three

A little later, Fird and Snyder heard someone crying. They stopped and listened. They followed the sound. It seemed to be coming from a clump of bushes. Fird peeked in. What he saw amazed him. There was a big clearing, with logs placed in the middle, like a large outdoor theater. The crying came from Hyenant—just an ordinary hyenant, party hyena, part ant—but he had on a lovely red coat and he was weeping something terrible.

Fird and Snyder went to see if they could help.

"Hello," said Fird. "Why are you crying? I thought hyenas were supposed to laugh a lot."

"Oh, *everybody* says that! *Everybody* says that!" wailed Hyenant. "Well, I don't. I don't know why I don't, but I don't. It takes a lot to even make me smile! But I cry over the silliest things. And once I start crying, I can't stop!" Then he bent double, crying great gobs of tears.

"Gee, that's terrible," said Fird. "Don't you know any good jokes?"

Crying Hyenant cried even harder. "No! But I do have a magic coat! And with this magic coat I can usually get someone to make me stop crying!"

"How's that?" asked Fird.

"By having a contest! You... you... !"

"I'm a fird," said Fird, "part fish, part bird. I'm looking for a herd of fird. Have you seen any?"

"No! No! Now, get out of the way. Out of the way! The contest is going to start!"

Fird suddenly wondered if he could get in the contest. If he could, he just might be able to get a fird out of
that magic coat.

"Can I be in the contest?" Fird blurted.

"No!" cried Hyenant. "Sign-ups ended yesterday!"

Just then music started to play. Fird and Snyder turned just in time to see several lovely woose glide out onto a beautiful pond. Oh, they were just ordinary woose—part worm, part goose—but they did a magnificent water ballet.

"Wooses' Song"

We are woose, part worm, part goose,
And we can make our necks so loose;
Not geese, not weese, we flock, not swarm;
A worm and goose, make woose, not gorm!

Then they all swam together in a big circle, to take a bow, but when they tried to swim apart, their long, wormlike necks got tangled up. They almost choked each other trying to get loose. Then, as they swam away, they kissed their lovely wings, and said, "Oh, he loved us. I just know he loved us!"

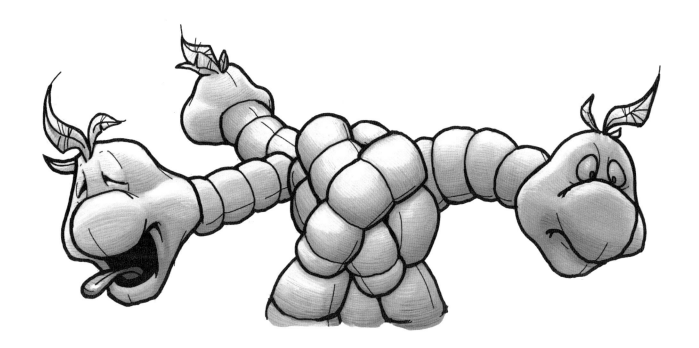

Fird and Snyder turned to the crying hyenant. He was still crying. Then, before anything else could happen, out pranced two wooly, shaggy shamels—just ordinary shamels, part sheep, part camels. They danced and strutted, and nodded and bowed as they sang. However, one shamel did have a bit of difficulty with his hump. It kept slipping, first to one side, then to the other. When it slipped it was no longer a hump but a lump. Embarrassed, he kept trying to keep it straight and balanced on his back.

"Shamel's Song"

Oh, we are shamels, can't you see?
Shamels, we happen to be;
Not sheep, not camels,
Just plain shamels,
Beautiful shamels, we.

But we've never seen in all our life
Such a weird concotion as you,
And we have seen many weird things;
Tell us, what do you do?

We sing, we dance,
In long wool pants,
We'll jump and smile at you;
Oh, please remain,
We'll make a game
Of trying to figure out you!

"I'm a fird!" said Fird. "Part fish, part bird! I'm looking for a herd of fird! Have you seen any?"

But the shamels didn't seem to even hear him. As they left they said, "Oh, he loved us. I just know he loved us!"

The shamels were barely out of sight when a couple of military-looking drid-ers marched out of the woods. They were ordinary driders—part dragon, part spiders—and it was obvious from the way they looked at Fird that they had never even heard of a fird. They wore fur hats and breathed smoke, and yet they weren't mean-looking driders. Immediately, they went into a fast and exciting dance.

Their many legs lifted and fell so quickly, they became a blur. They squatted and jumped, turned and twirled. And the faster they danced, the harder they breathed, and the harder they breathed, the hotter they smoked. Finally, great rolling flames shot out of their mouths. It burned their feet. That made them dance faster, which made them breathe hotter. Finally they had no choice— yelping and hollering, they ran for the pond.

Once their feet were cooled, they swam away, smiling and saying, "He loved us very much. I just know he loved us."

But Crying Hyenant had wept all through their song and was still weeping when they left. He sobbed so hard, it sounded as if his heart would surely break if he didn't stop.

Fird and Snyder supposed the show was over, when ever so slowly, up walked a blizzard—just an ordinary blizzard, part bird, part lizard. He was a strange, scroungy, two-feature creature who carried a beat-up, old guitar.

"Ah, Hyenant, sir," he began with a high, lisping voice. "Sir, are you ready for my song?"

Hyenant waved him away. "No more! No more! Go away!"

"But sir," said Blizard. "I signed up last week."

"Oh well... very well," gasped Hyenant. "Get on with it!"

Fird and Snyder watched, amazed, as Blizard walked over to a pile of muck and sticks and plopped down to sing. He strummed his broken guitar and suddenly a blizzard wind began to circle around him. Then it went out into the whole clearing. It threw leaves and twigs into the air. It picked up Snyder and blew him around in a circle. It dropped him at Hyenant's feet.

Hyenant immediately stopped crying and stared, dumbfounded.

"Why Is It?"

Why is it when we blink,
We don't say we have blunk?
And no one's been known to flink,
Although we often flunk?

Like some folk's hair just seem to kink,
Yet no one says it kunk;
And I don't even know I sleemp,
Although I'm told I slump.

Why, oh, why do I try?
Others would sit down and die;
At least they'd have a good cry,
But I… I try and I don't know why.

Is a little bit a hink
If a whole lot's a hunk?
Why don't folks admire my spink?
I'm told I've lots of spunk.

Oh, there must be a missing link
To which all words are lunk,
Or they are just a bunch of bink,
Though you may call it bunk!

Well, Hyenant started laughing almost immediately when Blizard started to sing. And before he was through, Hyenant was rolling on the ground, holding his sides, and yelling, "You win! You win, Blizard! You made me stop crying!"

All the other two-feature creatures in the contest rushed out to protest. They couldn't believe Blizard had won.

"He was terrible!" They yelled. "We were wonderful!"

"Yes, yes," said Hyenant, "You were wonderful, but he made me laugh! He asked such funny questions!"

"But he didn't mean to be funny!" complained a haughty shamel.

"Yes, I did," said Blizard. "I sat up all night practicing that song, just hoping it would make him smile."

"Well, now, Blizard, my boy," said Hyenant, "what do you want from my magic coat?"

Blizard grinned. "Tap shoes."

"Tap shoes!" quarreled the others. "Blizard you need so much! Why don't you get a new guitar? A new voice? Some new feathers?"

"Because I want tap shoes," said Blizard.

With a wide sweep of his hand, Hyenant reached into his magic coat. Then, with a sudden flourish, he brought it out, and said, "Ta-da!" On his hand was a pair of shiny black tap shoes.

"Oh, super! Just super!" said Blizard.

All the other two-feature creatures stomped off angrily.

Fird moved closer to Hyenant. He had to see if he could get a fird from that magic coat.

"Oh, Hyenant, sir. Could you grant me just one wish?"

Hyenant looked at him as if he had lost his mind. "Grant? *Grant?* I do not give away wishes! I scrimped and saved half my life for this coat!"

Fird nodded sadly. He glanced at Snyder. Snyder trembled because he thought Fird was going to give him away for a wish.

"No, no!" Fird comforted Snyder. "I would never trade you!"

Hyenant seemed touched by their friendship. "Oh, very well. Just one wish."

"I want a fird, like me."

"There's no such thing, I assure you." Just the same, Hyenant reached into his coat and brought out his hand with a loud "Ta-da!" But there was nothing there.

"See?" said Hyenant. "There's no such thing as a fird."

"I'm a fird!" protested Fird; but Hyenant just walked away.

Fird sighed. "Come on, Snyder. I guess it was silly to expect magic to solve my problem. Obviously, I'm going to have to keep looking."

Chapter Four

It was around noon when Fird and Snyder happened across a creek. There, they found bertles—just ordinary bertles, part bear, part turtles. They were passing the lazy afternoon rocking their bulky bear bodies in their great turtle shells, or floating in the creek on their backs, asleep.

"Well, looky here. Looky here," said one of the bertles.

"Looky what the cat drug up!"

"Hello," said Fird. "I'm a fird—part fish, part bird— and I'm looking for a herd of fird. Have you seen any?"

They shook their big bear heads and spun their shells around to look at Fird and Snyder. "Nope," said one bertle. "Never even heard of a fird. Saw a snog one time, though. Strangest thing I ever saw—a snog. Part snail, part hog. Yep, a snog it was all right.

Fird felt more and more disappointed. The bertles were obviously not going to be any help.

"Why do you want one?" asked another bertle.

"Because I am one," said Fird, "and I just want to know if I'm firding like a real fird."

"I never worried about how I was bertling," said another bertle. "I reckon I just am what I am. So I suggest you stop frettin' about firds and firding."

31

A young, happy-looking bertle picked up a jug and blew on it a couple of times. Another bertle picked up a washtub with a wire attached to it. Still another picked up an old scrub board. And they started to play.

"Whoever heard of a herd of fird?"

Whoever heard of a whole herd of fird?
Whoever heard of a Fird?
Whoever heard such a nerdy word?
The word is totally absurd.

Whoever heard of a Fird like you?
It is real disturbing.
Yes, we're disturbed, totally perturbed,
We've never even heard of firding!

One Fird. None Firds. Some Firds. A Herd!
One Fird, None Firds. Whoever heard of a Fird?

Why ain't you happy to be just what you is?
Since there's only one of you,
You get to say if you are Firding okay;
No one else even has a clue.

This is your time; it is your time to shine
But you need to realize:
Everything you need for you to succeed
Lies between your ears behind your eyes.

One Fird. None Firds. Some Firds A Herd!
One Fird, None Firds. Whoever heard of a Fird?

Then the bertles settled back into their comfortable shells. Fird frowned and said, "Well, I guess I'll just keep looking, because I do want to know if I'm firding okay!"

"Well, what for?" asked one of the older bertles. He reached to touch Snyder Spider, but Snyder hissed and jumped back. He made his hair stand straight out. The bertle drew back.

All the others laughed. This embarrassed the bertle and he said, "Like I always say, then you best just keep on moving, little Firdie. 'Cause we ain't about to get up and help you find a herd of fird."

Fird and Snyder moved past them. Snyder hissed again, just for the fun of it, but most of the bertles had already gone back to sleep.

"You know," said Fird, as they moved on down the creek bank, "sometimes I wish I could be more like the bertles." Snyder shivered and made a silly face.

"I mean it," argued Fird. "It sure would make life simpler if I just accepted what I saw and what I was told."

Snyder giggled and pointed a mocking finger at Fird.

He couldn't imagine Fird being that way.

Chapter Five

A little later, Fird and Snyder cast long, sad shadows as they moved across the darkening valley. Then a whiff of something delicious curled through the air and teased their noses. When they looked up, they saw a girouse. Oh, but she was no ordinary girouse—part giraffe, part mouse— she was a lovely, happy, two-feature creature.

She took a large, bubbling pot off a campfire.

"Good evening, gentlemen!" said Ms. Girouse. "You look plumb tuckered. How about a little supper?"

Fird and Snyder nodded and smiled. "That smells delicious!"

"Thank you." She quickly set them a place at the small, broken table. "Please, sit down."

As they ate, Fird told Ms. Girouse all about trying to find a herd of fird.

"I see," said Ms. Girouse, "and no one has ever heard of a fird."

"That's right," he sighed.

Ms. Girouse patted Snyder's head and Snyder came out of his chair, enjoying the pat. He ran up Ms. Girouse's long neck and slid down.

"Do you know where we should start looking for a herd of fird?" asked Fird. Ms. Girouse picked up a straw hat and cane. "Well, gentlemen, you must always start right where you are!"

"You Can't Sit Around"

You can't sit around thinkin' bout how hard it is,
Otherwise, you'll never get it did;
Can't sit around wishin' for the fishes to bite,
Gotta dig the worms instead.

Can't sit around hopin' for to be someone great,
Gotta start being today;
Can't sit around mopin', just thinking and a-hopin,
'Cause you'll never make it that way.

Can't sit around thinkin' that you aren't good enough,
'Less you wanna prove you really ain't!
Can't sit around blamin' other folks for your luck,
It's you who determines if you can or cain't!

So get up and get to it, now don't sit around,
Nothing ever chages that way;
Get up and get to it,
Prove that you can do it;
How 'bout getting' started today?

36

"Yeah!" Fird yelled. "You're right, Ms. Girouse! I know you're right. Thank you very much for dinner, but as you say... we can't sit around!"

"I understand." Ms. Girouse bowed politely. "Good luck!"

Fird and Snyder waved and danced happily away, feeling wonderful again.

Chapter Six

Soon, though, the valley became so dark, they decided to make a bed and sleep for the night. Snyder snuggled down into a soft mound of grass, next to Fird, but suddenly he jumped up again, twittering excitedly and pointing to lights in the distance.

"You're right," said Fird. "Maybe there's someone there who can help us. And we shouldn't just sit around."

Snyder nodded and ran off toward the lights. It was a long walk, all the way to the top of a tall hill, but finally they made it. There was a huge house with a large sign in front. Fird stepped back and read it aloud to Snyder. "Welcome all you poor and weary. Welcome all you homeless and hungry. Welcome all, welcome one. Welcome, welcome everyone."

"Wow!" said Fird. "These folks sound really nice!" Hurrying across the yard, they bounded up the porch. Fird knocked loudly and the door swung open almost at once.

"Yessss!" hissed a snooze—just an ordinary snooze, part snake, part mongoose. "Pleassse, come in!"

Fird and Snyder jumped back, frightened. "Ah... that's all right," stammered Fird. "We're... we're just looking for a herd of fird. Sorry to have bothered you."

"Pleassse!" hissed the snooze. "Come in!" And with that, the snooze grabbed them both and yanked them inside.

"Wait!" cried Fird. "We'll leave! We'll leave!"

"Never!" snapped the snooze. "You'll sssstay! You'll sssstay!" With lightning-fast movements, the snooze tossed Snyder into a cage, locked it, and threw it out the window. Next, she tossed Fird into a large room and locked the door.

Fird landed hard on his head. He blinked and looked around. Dozens of two-feature creatures stared at him.

"Wh-where am I?" he asked.

"You're in the snooses' prison!" said an old, tired two-feature creature. "And there's no escape!"

Fird frowned and stared at all the creatures sitting on their beds, looking dully at him. "Why are they holding us prisoner?"

"Because," said the old two-feature creature, "we are different from them. Snooses like only other snoozes. They do not like anyone who is different."

"Well, that's silly!" said Fird. "Everyone is different in some way." Fird glanced from one two-feature creature to another. "Why do you stay?" he asked. "Why don't you just leave?"

"You can't leave!" all the two-feature creatures shouted at once. "Once the snoozes have you, you can't leave! It just can't be done!"

"Don't say it can't be done!" Fird warned. "Don't say it can't be done!"

"But it can't!" they repeated. "It's never been done before!"

Fird stood as tall as he could, and with all the anger and determination he felt, he yelled, "Don't say it can't be done!"

"Reverse Psychology"

Don't say it can't be done!
Don't say it can't be done!

Just tell me that it can't be done,
Then stand back, watch me do it!
Say that something's really tough,
And I'll proceed to chew it!

Or say that's it's impossible,
And then I'll do it twice!
And if it's a gamble,
I'll get out my dice!

Reverse psychology! It works quite naturally.
Reverse psychology! It works reversibly!

Or say that something's easy and at once you know I'm frightened,
Or tell me it's not scary, and right then my fear is heightened.

Or say there's nothing to it,
And right then I'll surely freeze,
'Cause a sure thing always gives
Me rubber knees.

But if you say that any fool can do it,
Well, I'm no fool, as you can surely see!
My card's punched and I'm computed through it!
And the program reads, "Reverse Psychology"!

Reverse psychology! It works quite naturally!
Reverse psychology! It works reversibly!

Reverse, reverse, it works and works and works
And works until it hurts and hurts and hurts;
Reverse, reverse, reverse psychology!

Just then the door flew open. "What'sss going on in here?" yelled a snooze, grabbing Fird and slamming the door. He carried Fird down a long hallway, opened another door and pitched him in. Poor Fird tumbled down a rickety staircase and thudded to the floor.

"Troublemaker!" yelled the snooze as he stomped away.

Fird dusted himself off and looked around. He was in a basement.

Broken furniture and trash were piled everywhere. Bars covered the windows and cobwebs hung over everything.

Slowly, Fird went to the window. A tear slid down his face. "Snyder," he called, but no answer came. "Oh, Snyder, I miss you. I'm sorry I got you into this!"

Fird stared out at the darkness and cried, wondering if Snyder was okay, and if he should give up looking for a herd of fird.

"Isn't There Anyone?"

Isn't there anyone in the world
Who's ever felt like me?
Who's wondered who they are, and
Just why their life was meant to be?

But who do I turn to?
Who even cares?
Do I just sing to the wind?
And it takes my words
and just blows on by
And they're never heard again.

Isn't there anyone in the world
Who understands how I feel?
Who might share a hug,
or a word,
Who knows that my tears are real?

Too tired and sad to think or cry anymore, Fird leaned his little fird head on the window, and his little fird heart ached until he thought it would break.

Finally, he fell asleep.

On the other side of the house, Snyder Spider sat behind the locked cage door, crying for Fird.

Fird awoke the next morning to the sharp sound of a snoose's voice. "All right, you good-for-nothings! Get up and get to work!"

Fird glanced around quickly. He dashed up the stairs and climbed on a pile of boxes stacked beside the door. When the snooze poked her head in, Fird pounced on her!

She screeched for help. Fird darted down the hallway.

"Snyder! Snyder!" Fird screamed. "Come on!"

Other snoozes appeared. Fird shoved past them. He ran for the door. "Snyyyderrr!"

On the far side of the house, Snyder fought to get out of the cage. He banged against the bars. He bit them. He kicked them. He knew Fird was escaping, and he wanted to go, too!

Fird raced toward the bottom of the hill. The snoozes gave up. Fird was too fast for them.

"Snyder!" Fird screamed. "Snyder, where are you?"

When Fird realized he had run off and left his friend, he hung his head in shame. Life would never be the same without Snyder.

Poor Snyder; he wouldn't even be in this mess if Fird hadn't wanted to find a herd of fird. Fird felt worse than he'd ever felt in his whole life. What a terrible thing he had done to go off and leave Snyder.

But what Fird didn't know was that, back at the house, Snyder was still fighting, still trying to break free. Finally, he turned the cage over. It rolled on its side.

A snoose came running. "Get the sssspider! He'sss running away! And sssstealing our cage!"

Snyder whined and threw himself wildly about the cage. More snoozes ran toward him just as the cage door broke open! Snyder darted out. The snoozes knocked each other down, trying to catch him.

He shot past them like a streak of light.

Snyder didn't know Fird was coming back up the hill. Fird didn't know Snyder was coming down. And halfway up—or halfway down—they ran smack into each other.

It knocked them both stupid.

They hugged and kissed and jumped around. Oh, it was good to be together again! And so terrible to have been apart.

Chapter Seven

Fird laughed. "Well, I still wish I had found a herd of fird. I really do. Maybe if I just try one more time..."

Snyder looked horrified at the very thought of it.

Fird laughed, then threw back his little fird head and cupped his little fird wings around his little fird mouth, and yelled, *"Firds! Firds! I'm looking for a herd of fird!"*

Then the strangest thing happened. A little fird head popped out of a bush, then jumped back again. Fird and Snyder looked at each other. They both saw it!

Fird cupped his hands and yelled again. *"Firds! Firds! I'm looking for a herd of fird!"*

It happened again! Fird heads popped up from the bushes! Then suddenly they were everywhere!

There were firds and firds and firds! Everywhere they looked, firds were popping up and down out of the bushes. Hundreds of them! Thousands of them! Maybe even millions of them!

"Firds! Firds! Firds!" Fird jumped around, yelling with glee. "I finally found a herd of fird!"

He rushed up to the nearest fird. "Hello! I finally found a herd of fird!"

"No, you didn't," said the little fird.

Fird drew back in surprise. "What do you mean? Sure, I did! I'm a fird, part fish, part bird, and you're a fird—"

"No, no, no," said the fird. "I'm a *bish*, part bird, part fish. You're a bish. And all those things in the bushes are bishes."

"A... bish?" asked Fird. "A *bisssh*?"

The bish nodded soberly.

Snyder made a little chuckling, giggling sound. Then he laughed out loud. He laughed harder and harder, finally rolling on the ground. He kicked all eight of his feet and beat the ground with his hat. Fird had never heard him laugh so hard.

Embarrassed, Fird said, "All right, Snyder. That's enough!"

But try as he might, Snyder Spider couldn't stop laughing. After all they had been through, it was just too funny to find out fird was really a bish.

"So what do bishes do?" Fird finally asked.

The bish shrugged. "We bunch in the bushes."

"Why?" asked Fird.

"Because we're bishes."

Fird frowned. "Are you waiting for something?"

"Don't think so," said the bish. "We're just bunching."

Snyder laughed so hard, he cried. Fird tried to smile, but he couldn't. Finally, he snatched Snyder up by one leg and shook him. "Stop it, Snyder! Now, just stop it!"

Fird turned to the bish. "Well, do you sing... or dance... or *anything*?"

The bish dully shook his head. "Nope. We don't sing. We don't dance. We don't even play Monopoly. We just bunch."

Fird stared at him in disbelief. He just couldn't accept that he belonged to a group as boring as the bishes.

"So," said the bish, "if you're a bish, get in the bushes and start bunching!"

Snyder howled with delight. Fird gave him another yank. Then they both got into the bushes to bunch with the boring bishes. But the longer they stood there, the harder it was to be quiet. Snyder kept giggling. Fird grew more and more bored. He shifted from one foot to another, and a twig snapped. "Well, I finally found a herd of fird, and—!"

"Bishes! Bishes!" scolded the bishes. "You found a bunch of bishes. Now, be quiet! Bishes bunch quietly in the bushes!"

Fird sighed. It was no use. He could never just stand in the bushes, bunching with the boring bishes.

"Come on!" he said to Snyder. "Let's get out of here!"

But just then, faint crying sounds came from behind them. They turned to see. And there, pretty as a flower, was a little girl bish, her eyes all red from crying.

"Who are you?" asked Fird. "And, what's the matter?"

She wiped her eyes and sniffed. "I'm Belinda. And... well, I just keep having this feeling that there's something better than bunching in the bushes."

Snyder rolled his eyes and nodded as if to say, "Any fool can see that."

Belinda continued, "And I keep having this dream... "

"I Dream"

I dream a dream I love so much; all hearts gently touch
No tiny treasure, although small, is left to wither and fall.

I go on dreaming this dream of love
A dream that's so sweet
That's everything I'm dreaming of
It makes my life complete!
And so I dream... I dream.

Dreaming is such a lovely thing, helping the day go on,
Easing the sadness in between hours that seem so long.

I go on dreaming this dream of love
A dream that's so sweet,
That's everything I'm dreaming of
It makes my life complete!

And so I dream... I dream.
And so I dream... I dream.

Fird smiled. Just to look at her made his little fird heart do little fird flip-flops. "You know what?" he said. "There *is* such a place. I only just realized it while you were singing, but there *is* such a place! A place where you can be whatever you want to be, any time you want to be it!"

Belinda looked confused.

"Shhh!" scolded the bishes. "Bishes bunch quietly in the bushes!"

"It's all right!" Fird called to the bishes. "You bunch quietly in the bushes if you want! But I'm not a bish! I'm a fird!" And with that, he took Belinda's hand and led her out into the clearing. Snyder ran after them, glad to leave the bushes and the bishes.

"Now," said Fird, "about that place in your dreams..."

Belinda nodded. "Yes, it's a place where everyone can be just what they want to be, and do what they want to do—"

"Yes!" Fird interrupted. "I just realized there is such a place! It's right inside us! It's just *being* what we want to be, and *doing* what we want to do!"

"But I'm a bish," said Belinda. "Bishes just bunch in the bushes!"

"But they don't *have* to!" cried Fird. "And neither do you! They bunch because they want to. They could sing... they could dance... they could even play Monopoly! But they don't!"

Belinda smiled. "But you... you're a..."

Fird pulled himself up proudly. "I'm a fird! And it doesn't matter where I came from, or what I'm supposed to be! All that matters is where I'm *going*—and what I *do*!"

Snyder Spider sighed and rolled his eyes toward heaven, as if to say, "I thought he would never figured that out!"

"But you're a fird without a herd," said Belinda.

"Yes," said Fird. "I guess I am. But I'd rather be a fird without a herd than a boring bish, bunching in the bushes!"

"Me, too!" squealed Belinda. "Yeah! Me, too!"

And with that, Fird, Belinda, and Snyder left the boring bishes bunching in the bushes and danced happily across the valley, singing:

"I'm so glad to just be me..."

Whoever Heard of a Fird?

Othello Bach - Author

Othello Bach grew up in an orphanage. She didn't learn to read until the 8th grade -- and yet she has 18 published books. She graduated high school having read only two books.

Despite her humble beginnings, she wrote a bestselling novel House of Secrets at the age of 24 and sold it to Avon Books. Her next two popular novels sold to Zebra Books, and then she turned her attention to the challenging world of children's books.

She composed her first song at the age of eight, so it was only natural that many of her children's books included her original music and lyrics. She's had 37 songs recorded by stage and screen stars Joel Grey, Tammy Grimes, and four books recorded by Sandy Duncan.

www.othellobach.com

Shann Hurst - illustrator

Shann Hurst is a writer and illustrator born and raised in the Midwest who now makes his home on both coasts. Following a career as a freelance illustrator and fashion designer, he started Wish Engine Studio to develop new media children's storybooks without the general restraints associated with the publishing industry.

He is honored to have Othello Bach's "Whoever Heard of a Fird?" as his company's debut project.

www.wishenginestudio.com